The Adventures of Ruthie
and
a Little Boy Named Grandpa

The Adventures of Ruthie
and
a Little Boy Named Grandpa

~

Elliot Aronson & Ruth Aronson
with illustrations by Josette Nauenberg

iUniverse, Inc.
New York Lincoln Shanghai

The Adventures of Ruthie and a Little Boy Named Grandpa

Copyright © 2005 by Elliot Aronson

iUniverse books may be ordered through booksellers or by contacting:

iUniverse
2021 Pine Lake Road, Suite 100
Lincoln, NE 68512
www.iuniverse.com
1-800-Authors (1-800-288-4677)

ISBN-13: 978-0-595-36656-9 (pbk)
ISBN-13: 978-0-595-81079-6 (ebk)
ISBN-10: 0-595-36656-2 (pbk)
ISBN-10: 0-595-81079-9 (ebk)

Printed in the United States of America

The Adventures of Ruthie
and
a Little Boy Named Grandpa

"Grandpa, please tell me a story," Ruthie said.

"OK," said Grandpa. "What shall it be? Hansel and Gretel? Jack and the Beanstalk? Goldilocks and the Three Bears?"

"No, no, no," said Ruthie, who was six years old and very beautiful and very smart. "You've told me those stories a zillion times, and they are so boring."

Grandpa, who was 71 years old and cranky, sighed deeply and said, "So you've heard all the stories. What should I do?"

"Make something up," said Ruthie.

"Okay," said Grandpa. "How about if I told you a story about Grandpa as a little boy?"

"Goody," exclaimed Ruthie. "But can I be part of the story?"

"I don't see how," said Grandpa. "When I was a little boy, you hadn't even been born yet."

"Make it up," said Ruthie.

Grandpa scratched his head, stroked his beard, and rubbed his nose.

"Hmmm," he said. "Okay. The name of this story is 'The Adventures of Ruthie and a Little Boy Named—um, um— Grandpa.'"

§

Once upon a time Ruthie and her friend Grandpa were taking a walk in the woods. It was getting dark.

"I'm scared," said Grandpa. "Let's go back home. We might get losted."

"Oh, don't be such a baby," said Ruth. "Let's go just a little bit farther."

After a few minutes, it began to rain.

"I'm getting wet," said Grandpa. "Let's go home."

"Look," said Ruthie. "There's a little cottage. Let's go in until it stops raining."

Ruthie boldly approached the door and knocked three times. Rap. Rap. Rap. There was no response. Ruthie waited for a minute and then knocked again. Rap. Rap. Rap.

Then, very slowly, the door began to open. There stood a little old woman.

The old woman said, "Oh, children, how good to see you. I've been waiting a very long time for someone to visit me. I am so lonely. Come in, come in, it's raining outside. Come and sit by the oven and warm yourself. Take off your wet clothes and dry them by the oven."

Ruthie and Grandpa took off their wet clothes and sat shivering by the oven.

"What is your name, little girl?" the woman asked.

"Ruthie," said Ruthie.

"What a pretty name!"

"And what is your name, little boy?"

"My name is Grandpa."

The old woman looked puzzled and thought, "What a peculiar name for a little boy."

Grandpa whispered to Ruthie, "This old woman looks very familiar. I'm sure I've seen her somewhere before."

"Oh, pshaw," said Ruthie. "We have never been in the forest. How could we have possibly seen this woman?"

Then the old woman said, "Ruthie, I have a cake and some cookies baking in the oven. They may be almost done. I am getting old and feeble. It hurts me to bend over. Would you kindly open the oven door, lean in, and see if the cake and cookies are done?"

Just then, Grandpa grabbed Ruthie by the arm and said to the old woman, "Please excuse us, but we need to have a conference."

He then led Ruthie into a corner of the cottage. He whispered, "Ruthie, Ruthie. Don't go near the oven. I just remembered where I saw the old woman. She might be a witch. She was in a story, and in that story she tried to push a little girl into the oven and bake her!"

Ruthie said, "Oh, pshaw, Grandpa. She's a very nice old woman. You need to be more trusting."

Ruthie opened the oven door and stuck her head way inside while the woman stood behind her peering over her shoulder.

Grandpa was so frightened that he closed his eyes and covered them with his hands. He could not bear to watch.

Then Ruthie said, "I think that the cake and the cookies are baked enough."

"No! No!" said Grandpa.

Ruthie took a long paddle and reached into the oven and took the cookies and cake out of the oven.

Grandpa gradually uncovered his eyes and saw Ruthie and the old woman eating the cake and the cookies and finally asked, "May I have some, too?"

The old woman said, "Please join us. I believe in eating dessert before dinner. Don't you?"

Ruthie and Grandpa jumped for joy.

"Yippee!" they shouted, happy to have found a grownup who agreed with them.

The old woman then brought out some ice cream. All three ate to their heart's content.

By then, Ruthie's and Grandpa's clothes were dry, and they got dressed.

Then the old woman said, "And now for the main course."

She went to the cupboard and brought out a bowl that contained three large eggs. She cracked them open and made an omelet.

Ruthie and Grandpa were not very hungry anymore, but when they tasted the omelet, they discovered that it was the most delicious omelet they had ever eaten.

Ruthie said, "Where did you get such large, delicious eggs?"

The old woman said, "I have a goose in the backyard who lays these eggs. Perhaps you have heard of the goose that lays golden eggs. But my goose is much better than that. One cannot eat golden eggs, but one can certainly eat delicious eggs."

"Can we see the goose?" asked Ruthie.

Before the woman could answer, Grandpa said, "Ruthie, it's getting dark. I think it's time to go home, because we might have a hard time finding our way."

Ruthie answered by saying, "Oh, Grandpa. It will only take a minute."

Grandpa said, "Well, okay."

The old woman led Ruthie and Grandpa into the backyard.

"Here, goose. Here, goose," the old woman called.

But there was no response.

"Here, goose. Here, goose. Oh, my goodness! My goose seems to have disappeared!" said the old woman.

Just then, Grandpa looked up and saw at the top of a very tall tree something white that looked like a goose. He said, "Is that your goose?"

The old woman said, "Oh, yes, it is...Goose, come down, come down."

But the goose was too frightened.

Then Ruthie said, "Grandpa and I will climb the tree and bring the goose down."

"Are you sure you can do it?" asked the old woman.

"Yes," said Ruthie.

"NO!" said Grandpa.

"Let's try," Ruthie said to Grandpa.

And they began to climb the tree.

When they were halfway up the tree, Ruthie said to Grandpa, "You see how easy it is! You should be more trusting."

"Yes," said Grandpa. "You are right. We can climb up the tree, but are you sure we can climb down again?"

"Oh, pshaw," said Ruthie.

When they reached the top of the tree, Grandpa reached out to take hold of the goose. But the goose was frightened and pecked Grandpa's finger.

"Ouch!" cried Grandpa, pulling his hand away.

Ruthie reached out and put her hand around the goose's beak. With her other hand she patted the goose gently on the head and said, "Dear goose, we are not going to harm you. We are trying to help you come down from the tree. Don't be afraid. We will be very gentle with you. If I let go of your beak, do you promise not to peck at us?"

"Honk, honk," said the goose, and nodded.

Ruthie let go of the beak, and the goose nestled into her arms. Ruthie and Grandpa then started to climb down the tree. But when Ruthie looked down and saw how high up they were, her legs began to tremble.

"Oh, Grandpa," she said. "You were right. It is easier to climb up than to climb down. What shall we do?"

"I don't know," said Grandpa. "We might be up here forever."

Just then, Ruthie saw a very tall man walking through the forest with an ax over his shoulder.

"Oh, look," said Ruthie. "Let's ask him to help us."

"No, no, no," said Grandpa. "That's not a man. That's a giant! Don't you remember that story about Jimmy and the beanstalk? I think there was a giant with an ax who chopped down the beanstalk while Jimmy was on top of it, and Jimmy fell down and broke his crown."

"No, no, no," said Ruthie. "You've got it all wrong. First of all, the little boy's name was Jack, not Jimmy. And it was Jack who chopped down the beanstalk while the giant was on top of it. And the Jack who fell down and broke his crown is in a different story."

"Whatever," said Grandpa. "Giants are evil anyway, and he might hurt us."

"Oh, pshaw," said Ruthie. "He's not a giant. He's only a tall man."

Ruthie shouted, "Oh, Mister, Mister Tall Man. Would you help us come down from this tree?"

"Certainly," said the tall man.

He lifted his ax from his shoulder.

"Oh, no," said Grandpa. "He's going to cut down the tree."

But the tall man cut a few branches from a neighboring tree, took a hammer and nails out of his pocket, and built a ladder, which he put against the tree.

Ruthie, Grandpa, and the goose scampered down the ladder. While they were scampering, Ruthie said, "You see, Grandpa. You really should be more trusting!"

When they reached the bottom of the ladder, they were very happy. They held hands and began to dance—Ruthie, Grandpa, the Very Tall Man Who Wasn't a Giant, and the goose.

The old woman joined them, and they danced and they danced and they danced.

The goose was so excited that she began to lay eggs—one after another, until there was a huge pile of eggs. The old woman invited all the people into the house. She filled three bags of eggs and gave the tall man, Ruthie, and Grandpa each a bag to take home with them.

Ruthie and Grandpa started to walk through the forest, but by now it was dark, and they weren't sure which way to go.

Grandpa yelled, "Mr. Giant. Oops, I mean Mr. Tall Man. Would you please do us a favor and lead us to the edge of the forest so that we can find our way home?"

"Certainly," said the tall man.

Ruthie bent down and whispered into Grandpa's ear: "Aren't you afraid that he might lead us deeper into the forest and kill us and eat us?"

Grandpa smiled and said: "I've learned one thing during this adventure: not to judge people by how they look."

"I've learned something too," said Ruthie. "Not to climb up without having a clear idea about how I am going to get back down!"

Just then the tall man stretched out his huge arms and put one of his hands on Ruthie's head and the other on Grandpa's head. "Here we are, children," he said, "at the edge of the forest. And if I am not mistaken, those two houses across the meadow are yours."

"Yes! Yes!" exclaimed Ruthie and Grandpa, jumping with joy.

They both hugged the tall man, waved goodbye, and ran home, where they were greeted by their mothers and fathers who were eager to hear all about their adventures.

THE END

978-0-595-36656-9
0-595-36656-2